Make sure to find all the TOON books by Liniers:
The Big Wet Balloon, **A *PARENTS MAGAZINE* TOP TEN!**
Written and Drawn by Henrietta, **A BOLOGNARAGAZZI AWARD WINNER!**
Good Night, Planet, **AN EISNER AWARD WINNER!**

TOON LEVEL TWO

For Matilda, Clementina, and Emma

Editorial Director: FRANÇOISE MOULY

Book Design: FRANÇOISE MOULY & RICARDO LINIERS SIRI

RICARDO LINIERS'S artwork was done using India ink and watercolor.

A TOON Book™ © 2021 Liniers & TOON Books, an imprint of RAW Junior, LLC, 27 Greene Street, New York, NY 10013. No part of this book may be used or reproduced in any manner whatsoever without written permission except in the case of brief quotations embodied in critical articles and reviews. TOON Graphics™, TOON Books®, LITTLE LIT®, and TOON Into Reading!™ are trademarks of RAW Junior, LLC. All rights reserved. All our books are Smyth Sewn (the highest library-quality binding available) and printed with soy-based inks on acid-free, woodfree paper harvested from responsible sources.

Library of Congress Cataloging-in-Publication Data: Names: Liniers, 1973- author, illustrator. Title: Wildflowers : a Toon book / by Liniers. Description: First edition. | New York : TOON Books, [2021] | Audience: Ages up to 8. | Audience: Grades 2-3. | Summary: Sisters embark on an adventure of the imagination through the jungles of a mysterious island, which reveals the unbreakable bond they share. Identifiers: LCCN 2020042466 | ISBN 9781943145539 (hardcover) Subjects: LCSH: Graphic novels. | CYAC: Graphic novels. | Sisters--Fiction.| Adventure and adventurers--Fiction. | Imagination--Fiction. Classification: LCC PZ7.7.L56 Wil 2021 | DDC 741.5/973--dc23   Printed in China by C&C Offset Printing Co., Ltd. Distributed to the trade by Consortium Book Sales & Distribution, a division of Ingram Content Group; orders (866) 400-5351; ips@ingramcontent.com; www.cbsd.com.

ISBN 978-1-943145-53-9   (hardcover edition)
ISBN 978-1-943145-54-6   (hardcover special gift edition)
21 22 23 24 25 26 C&C 10 9 8 7 6 5 4 3 2 1

WWW.TOON-BOOKS.COM

8

11

12

13

14

15

29

34

ABOUT THE AUTHOR

"As soon as I took this photo of my three young daughters looking at the jungle in the Yucatan, Mexico, I began to imagine this book," says RICARDO LINIERS SIRI about the moment inspiration struck. "Matilda, Clementina, and Emma, 'You belong among the wildflowers,' as the song by Tom Petty goes. Thank you for all that you brought to this story, and thanks to your friend, Paz Babineau, for helping me find the tiny gorilla."

Liniers's U.S. debut, *The Big Wet Balloon*, was selected as one of *Parents Magazine*'s Top Ten, and his second book starring his girls, *Good Night, Planet*, was the winner of the Eisner Award for Best Comics for Beginning Readers. This third book completes the set of the author's ode to his three daughters. Originally from Buenos Aires, Argentina, the family is now happily inhabiting the mysterious jungles of Vermont.